For my father

T.W.-J.

For P.A. and K.M.

I.W.

First published in Canada 1988 by Groundwood Books

Text copyright © 1988 by Tim Wynne-Jones
Illustrations copyright © 1988 by Ian Wallace

Margaret K. McElderry Books
Macmillan Publishing Company
866 Third Avenue
New York, NY 10022

First United States Edition

Design by Michael Solomon
Printed and bound in Hong Kong
by Everbest Printing Company, Ltd.

10 9 8 7 6 5 4 3 2 1

Library of Congress Cataloging-in-Publication Data

Wynne-Jones, Tim.
Builder of the moon.

Summary: Brave block-builder David Finebloom
receives a message from the moon that it is falling
apart and rushes off to help.
[1. Blocks (Toys) — Fiction.   2. Moon — Fiction.]
I. Wallace, Ian, 1950-   ill. II. Title.
PZ7.W993Bu   1988   [E]   88-12703

ISBN 0-689-50472-1

BUILDER OF THE MOON

by Tim Wynne-Jones
pictures by Ian Wallace

Margaret K. McElderry Books
NEW YORK

A message arrived from outer space,

a message from the Moon.

Help! I'm falling apart. Yours, the Moon.

Luckily it arrived at the home
of brave block-builder
David Finebloom.

David waved from his window.
"Don't worry, Moon."

He gathered all the things he would need
for a busy night's work
and told his mom not to wait up.

Back in his room he laid out
a launch pad and turned the dial to Moon.
He activated his spaceship and

Whooosh! He was off.

He arrived just in time and

started right in. First the floor
of the tranquil sea,

then the valleys, hills and mountains.
He had brought all the right shapes and
all the right colors.

Bigger, bigger, bigger grew the Moon,
and rounder, too.
Course upon course, layer upon layer,
until

it was done; it was full.
Hurray for David Finebloom!

It was a little rough in places,

but who on Earth would notice.

David waved from his spaceship.
"Don't worry, Mom!" He set the dial for
home and got there just in time for

breakfast on the porch.
A perfect five-minute boiled egg.